This book
belongs to

_____

_____

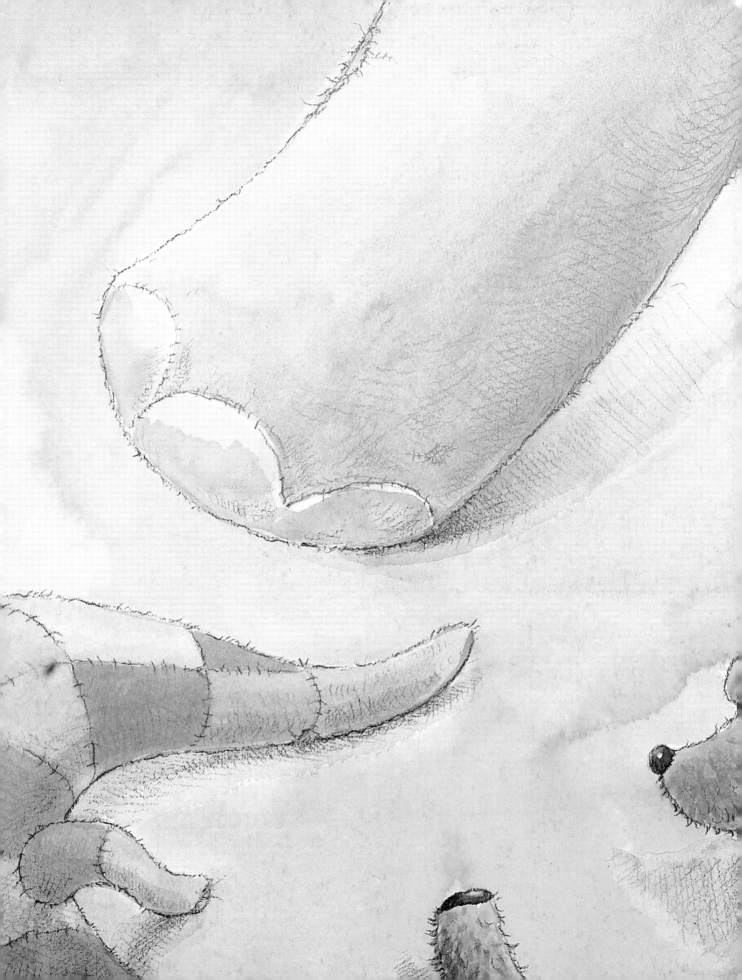

To Rosie and Eve
G.R.

To Ted, my old art teacher
and, as ever, my wonderful wife, Tiziana
J.B-B.

First published in Great Britain in 2006 by Gullane Children's Books
This paperback edition published in 2007 by
Gullane Children's Books
an imprint of Pinwheel Limited
Winchester House, 259-269 Old Marylebone Road,
London NW1 5XJ

1 3 5 7 9 10 8 6 4 2

Text © Gillian Rogerson 2006
Illustrations © John Bendall-Brunello 2006

The right of Gillian Rogerson and John Bendall-Brunello to be identified as the author and illustrator of this work
has been asserted by them in accordance with the Copyright, Designs and Patents Act, 1988.
A CIP record for this title is available from the British Library.

ISBN-13: 978-1-86233-655-1
ISBN-10: 1-86233-655-5

Printed and bound in China

The Teddy Bear SCARE

rrroar

Gillian Rogerson ● John Bendall-Brunello

GULLANE
CHILDREN'S BOOKS

"Why do I have to be cute
and cuddly?" asked Ted.
"Because you're a teddy bear.
That's your job." said T-Rex.

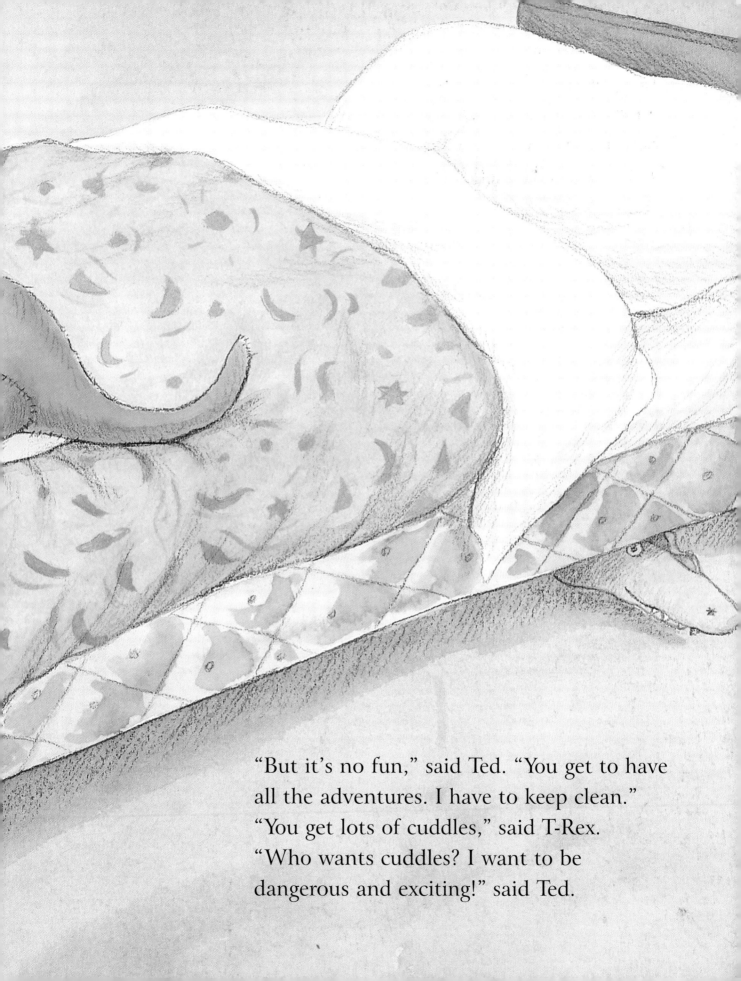

"But it's no fun," said Ted. "You get to have all the adventures. I have to keep clean."
"You get lots of cuddles," said T-Rex.
"Who wants cuddles? I want to be dangerous and exciting!" said Ted.

He jumped off the bed and dived into the toy box. He found Lion.
"Teach me how to roar like you," said Ted.

"Okay,"
said Lion.

ROAR!

rrroar

said Ted.

Lion laughed and patted Ted on the head. "You're so sweet," he said.

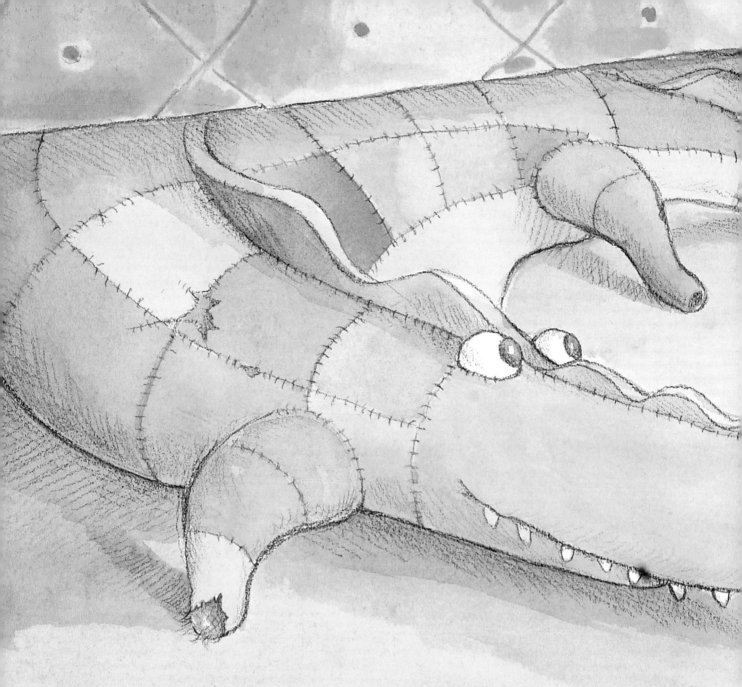

Ted climbed out of the toy box and squeezed under
the bed. He saw two big eyes looking at him and
two rows of very large, sharp teeth.
"Crocodile, can you show me how to grin like you?"
asked Ted.
"Of course," said Crocodile. "Think of something
huge and delicious that you'd like to eat."

Ted thought of a jam sandwich. He opened
his mouth wide and bared his little teeth.
Crocodile chuckled. "What a lovely smile.
You look so cute."

Ted came out from
under the bed and
sat down to think.
He leant against a box.
"BOO!"

It was Jack-in-the-box.
"You scared me," said Ted. "Do it again."
So Jack did.
That's what I'll do, thought Ted.

He hid behind the box and waited. He
saw Elephant and Zebra walking past.
He jumped out and shouted, "BOO!"

Elephant and Zebra smiled at each other.
"Isn't he adorable," said Elephant.
"I just want to cuddle him," said Zebra.
"Don't you dare cuddle me," said Ted.
"I'm not that kind of bear anymore."

Ted stomped back towards the toy box.
He didn't see the toy train on the floor –
until he tripped over it!

Ted flew through the air and
landed head-first between the
toy box and the wardrobe.

Mmmfff!

Ted wiggled free. There was something stuck over his face. Ted pulled at it. It wouldn't move. "Mmmfff!" cried Ted. His voice sounded funny.

Ted saw Lion and ran over to ask for help.
Lion didn't know it was Ted. It looked like a scary monster.
Lion opened his mouth to roar. But his roar was too scared
to come out. Lion ran away.

Ted ran towards Crocodile and shouted, "Mmmfff!"
Help! thought Crocodile when he saw
the monster. He showed his sharp teeth
to frighten the monster away.

mmmmff!

But his teeth chattered
with fright and
wouldn't stop.
Crocodile ran away.

What's wrong with them?
thought Ted.
He saw the other toys and
waved to them. The toys
screamed and ran away.

Jack-in-the-box jumped
back in his box and
shouted, "I'm not in!"

Ted was puzzled.
Then he saw something in the
wardrobe mirror. He looked closer.
It was horrible!
It was terrible!
It was Ted!
Ted grinned. *This is good*, he thought.
He tried to pull the mask off.
It still wouldn't move.

This is bad, thought Ted. *I don't want to be scary* all *the time.* He looked around the empty room. Had he scared his friends away forever?

The bedroom door banged open. Lucy
ran in and grabbed her skipping rope.
She saw Ted on the floor and picked him up.

"You silly bear," she laughed.
She took the mask off and put
Ted back on the floor.

She ran out of the bedroom,
slamming the door behind her.

One by one, the other toys
came out of their hiding places.

"Was that horrible monster really you?" asked Lion.

Ted nodded.

"I was so frightened," said Crocodile.

"I will never call you cute and cuddly again," said Elephant.

The toys still felt a bit scared. They looked at Ted.

"Are we still friends?" asked Ted.
"Of course," said the toys.
"Is it okay if we hug you?" asked Zebra.
"Just a little hug," said Ted.
The toys crowded around Ted
and hugged him tight.

Ted smiled and hugged them back.

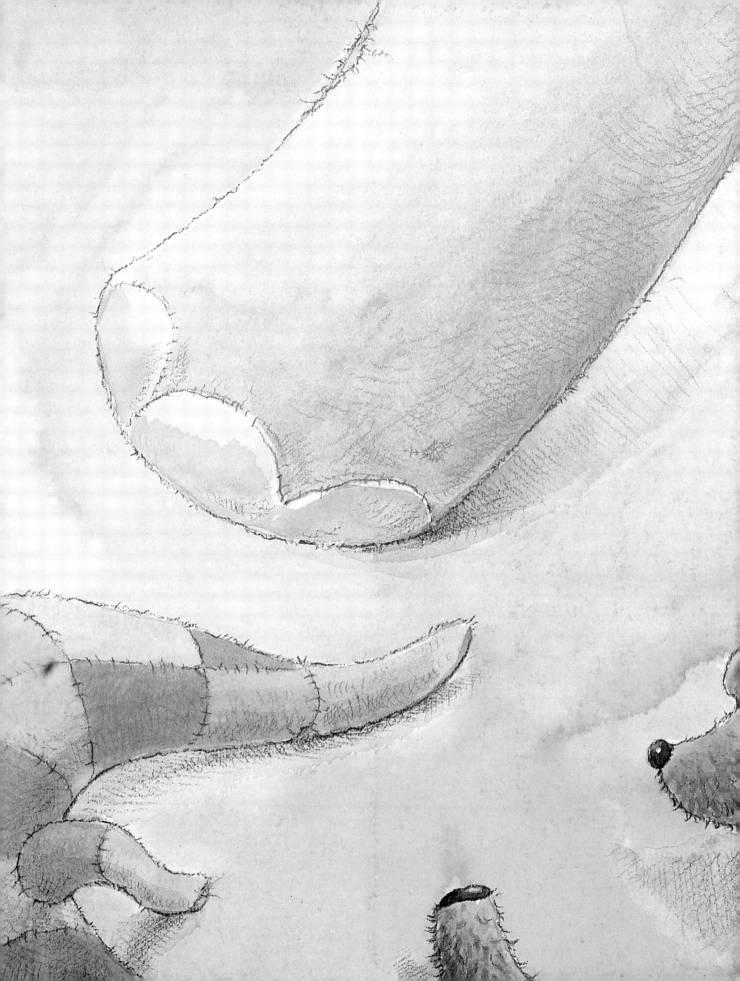

Other Gullane Children's Books
for you to enjoy...

Pugwug and Little
SUSIE JENKIN-PEARCE •
TINA MacNAUGHTON

Very Interesting!
YOKOCOCO

Little Lion Lost!
MARK MARSHALL

We Love the Snow
RICHARD EDWARDS • JOHN WALLACE

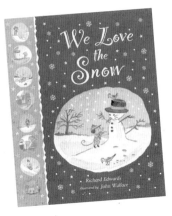